Beth's Job

Carole Roberts

Illustrated by Michael Garland

Green Light Readers

sandpiper

Houghton Mifflin Harcourt

Boston New York 2009

It's the day for new jobs.

"What is my job?" asks Beth.

“You can water the plant,”

says Mr. Hall.

Oh, no, thinks Beth.

Max helps with Hops.

Hops is the class pet.

I want that job, thinks Beth.

Ann helps with the eggs.

Beth wants that job.

Jeff is first in line.

Beth wants that job, too.

Glen gets to hold the flag.

I want to hold the flag,

thinks Beth.

I don't like this plant, thinks Beth.

I want a new job.

"Look at this flower, Beth!"

says Mr. Hall.

“Oh, my!” says the class.

"Oh, my!" says Beth.

"How did that get there?"

“This job is the best!”

Beth likes her job at last!

ACTIVITY

What Do You Think?

How does Beth feel about her job when the story begins? How does she feel at the end? Why?

Why do you think Beth wants to help with the eggs?

How does Beth's job make the classroom a better place?

Write about a job you enjoy doing. Tell why that job is important.

Meet the Illustrator

Michael Garland has written and illustrated many books for children. He spent his childhood in New York exploring the woods, playing sports, and drawing. Drawing was the thing he did best.

www.sandpiperbooks.com

First Green Light Readers edition 2009

Green Light Readers and its logo are trademarks of Houghton Mifflin Harcourt Publishing Company.

SANDPIPER and the SANDPIPER logo are trademarks of Houghton Mifflin Harcourt Publishing Company.

Library of Congress Cataloging-in-Publication Data
Roberts, Carole (Carole Jennifer)
Beth's job/Carole Roberts; illustrated by Michael Garland.
p. cm.
"Green Light Readers."
Summary: After getting a new job in her classroom, Beth takes a while to decide whether or not she likes it.
[1. Schools—Fiction.] I. Garland, Michael, 1952– ill. II. Title.
PZ7.R5403Be 2009
[E]—dc22 2008006886

ISBN 978-0-15-206710-6
ISBN 978-0-15-206716-8 (pb)

A C E G H F D B
A C E G H F D B (pb)

Manufactured in China

Ages 4–6

Grade: K–1

Guided Reading Level: D

Reading Recovery Level: 5

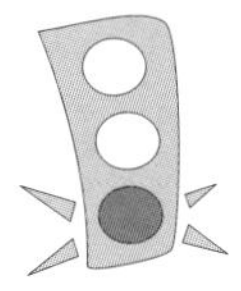

Green Light Readers

For the reader who's ready to GO!

"A must-have for any family with a beginning reader."—*Boston Sunday Herald*

"You can't go wrong with adding several copies of these terrific books to your beginning-to-read collection."—*School Library Journal*

"A winner for the beginner."—*Booklist*

Five Tips to Help Your Child Become a Great Reader

1. Get involved. Reading aloud to and with your child is just as important as encouraging your child to read independently.

2. Be curious. Ask questions about what your child is reading.

3. Make reading fun. Allow your child to pick books on subjects that interest her or him.

4. Words are everywhere—not just in books. Practice reading signs, packages, and cereal boxes with your child.

5. Set a good example. Make sure your child sees YOU reading.

Why Green Light Readers Is the Best Series for Your New Reader

- Created exclusively for beginning readers by some of the biggest and brightest names in children's books
- Reinforces the reading skills your child is learning in school
- Encourages children to read—and finish—books by themselves
- Offers extra enrichment through fun, age-appropriate activities unique to each story
- Incorporates characteristics of the Reading Recovery program used by educators
- Developed with Harcourt School Publishers and credentialed educational consultants

E 8/10
R (yellow)